Hi, my name is Kathy and for 23 years I was a teacher reading wonderful stories to children in my class. Children like my own girls, Daisy and Poppy, and children just like you! I thought I would write a book myself, and I hope that it will be read in schools and homes all over the world. I hope you enjoy this magical story.

AUSTIN MACAULEY PUBLISHERS™

LONDON * CAMBRIDGE * NEW YORK * SHARJAH

Summer Santa

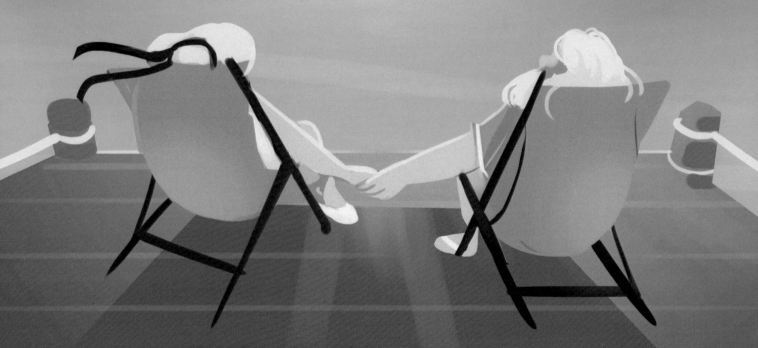

Kathy Smith-Summers

A CIP catalogue record for this title is available from the British Library.

ISBN 9781398460690 (Paperback)
ISBN 9781398460706 (ePub e-book)

www.austinmacauley.com

First Published 2023
Austin Macauley Publishers Ltd®
1 Canada Square
Canary Wharf
London
E14 5AA

To my wonderful children, Daisy and Poppy, my fantastic husband Steve, and the amazing friends and family that have supported me in so many ways.

To Matt and Marc for your kind donation.

I would also like to thank Alison Bailey for helping with Proof Reading and Angela Timmons and Steve Summers for their generous donations

"I'm bored!" said Santa. It was July 2nd and Santa has been 'relaxing' for 6 months.

"Why don't you do a jigsaw?" said Mrs Santa.

"Done them all," said Santa.

"Play a game on the iPad?"

"Finished them all," said Santa.

"What about Sudoku?"

"I'm not very good at that," said Santa, glumly.

"Well, I don't know then!" said Mrs Santa, she looked outside and had an idea. "Why don't you go on your beach trike and have a ride along the beach front? Perhaps it will give you some inspiration."

So Santa put on his beach hat, t-shirt and shorts, slapped on some sunscreen and climbed onto his trusty old trike. The trike was old and rusty, the leather on the seat was split and a bit uncomfortable when it went over a bumpy bit of the promenade! But Santa loved to get out in the fresh air, especially after spending the winter in the workshop.

It was a beautiful summer's day and as Santa peddled past, he smiled to himself as he saw the children playing happily on the beach. They had buckets and spades and were digging holes and burying each other in the sand. As he watched an idea started to dawn on him. What if there was another celebration a bit like Christmas? What if in the middle of the year children had an extra gift? Something to keep them from getting bored? Not boring jigsaws or tricky Sudoku but something that they could create from shells and seaweed? An idea started to form in Santa's head. He raced home and burst through the beach hut door.

"I've got it!" he exclaimed. "We are going to have a summer celebration, a day where every child will get a gift to stop them getting bored like I did, and it will remind them that it is half way to Christmas. Something to make and to keep forever and YOU are going to be the one to deliver it!"

"ME???" said Mrs Claus.

"Yes!" said Santa. "All year you support me and put up with my grumbling and groaning about the run up to Christmas. You mend my suit and make my cocoa and look after me and the elves, and you never get any of the praise. It's always Santa this and Santa that. Well, this time it will be your turn to have the limelight! What do you think??" Mrs Santa looked shocked at first, and then she thought and then she broke out into a wide grin!

"Yes!" she said. "I think you're on to something, but how will we work it? How will people know?"

"Well we will start small. Just local for this year, perhaps here in Sutton-on-Sea. And then we will see how it goes."

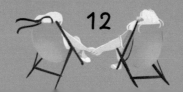

So Santa and Mrs Claus spent all day and all night planning what they would do. They collected hundreds of shells from the beach in many different colours, shapes and sizes. The scoured the sand and found some smooth, shiny, sparkling sea glass. They collected dried seaweed and bits of old fishing nets that the children could thread things onto. They created 'how to' booklets so the children would know what to do with the things that they got and then packed them all into small seaside themed boxes. The next morning, they had made enough boxes for all the children in Sutton. Santa already had a list of all the local children's names and addresses that he used at Christmas so he printed it out and attached a map. Then with a little touch of Santa's magic, they made the beach trike bigger and better, the rust disappeared and there was a comfy seat for Mrs Claus to sit on and with a last flourish of magic dust, Santa made the beach trike fly!

Mrs Claus put on her best red and white summer dress and a bit of sparkle for her hair and she was ready for the off. "You look wonderful," said Santa. "Here's the finishing touch!" Santa had made her a magic summer beach bag to match her dress. He put all the presents in there and gave her the list.

"I'm a bit nervous," said Mrs Claus." I've never done this before!"

"You will be as amazing as you always are," said Santa with a big beaming smile. He gave Mrs Claus a kiss on the forehead then a big hug and a squeeze and said, "Good luck dear," and Mrs Claus got on the trike and cycled away.

Dropping off the presents was easy. She just popped them through each letter box. No magic chimney needed for these small surprises! She made sure the names on the boxes matched the address on the list and ticked everyone off as she went (she had always been the most organised of the couple). That day she worked for 12 hours making sure each gift was delivered. Peddling down alleyways and sweeping through sand dunes. Flying up high to reach flats and floating to children who lived on boats and canals!

She had so much fun that she was a little sad when she finally delivered the last present. As she pushed it through the door, she realised how Santa must feel at the end of every Christmas Day. She was exhausted but exhilarated at the thought of happy faces waking up to a surprise gift the next day.

As she slowly peddled her way up the drive and went through the door, she saw Santa waiting for her, just as she did for him every December 25th. He had a cold glass of orange juice and a cheese sandwich ready for her, her favourite. As she ate and drank, she sat on the bed and smiled. What a wonderful day it had been.

She lay on the bed and fell fast asleep, not even finishing her food. Santa looked at her with love and pride and knowing now how she felt about him after he had finished his Christmas delivery.

The next morning excited cries and surprised laughter rang across Sutton-on-Sea. Children opened their boxes and enjoyed making their gifts that day.

Santa and Mrs Claus sat outside their beach hut in their deck chairs and watched the happy faces of the children as they showed each other the things they had made. They looked at each other with satisfaction and knew that they had, in their own special way, made the world a better place. It was the very first 'halfway mas'

THE END